DATE DUE

JUL 0 1 2009			

Demco, Inc. 38-293

D1256983

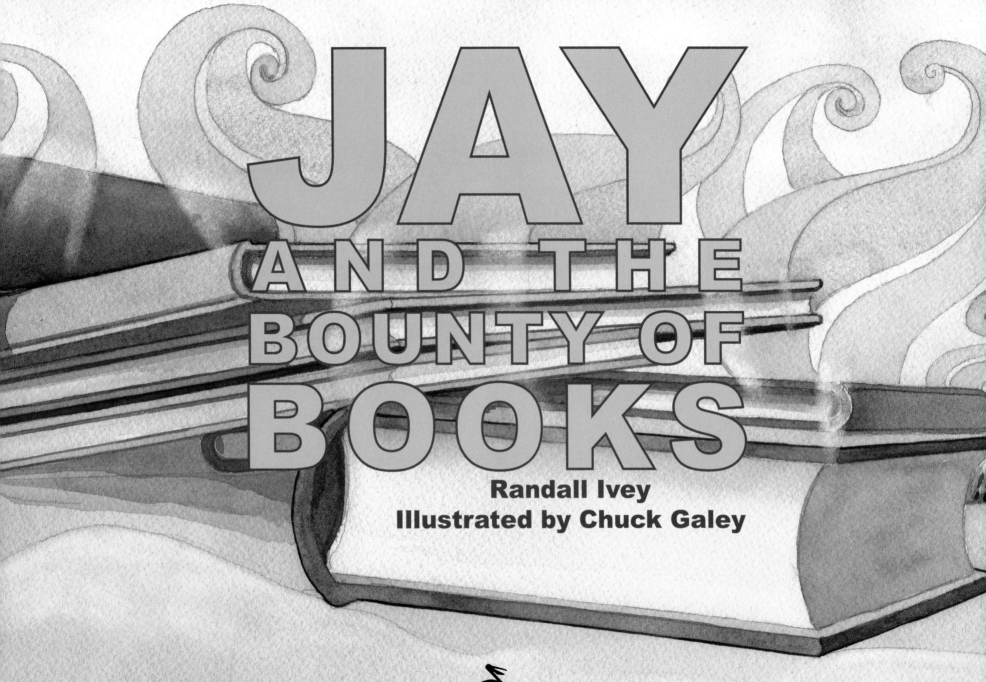

JAY
AND THE
BOUNTY OF
BOOKS

Randall Ivey

Illustrated by Chuck Galey

PELICAN PUBLISHING COMPANY
GRETNA 2007

With much love, to my nephew, Jay Cunningham—R. I.
For Bill and Terry; brothers forever—C. G.

The word "Pelican" and the depiction of a pelican are trademarks
of Pelican Publishing Company, Inc., and are registered in the
U.S. Patent and Trademark Office.

Library of Congress Cataloging-in-Publication Data

Ivey, Randall.
  Jay and the bounty of books / by Randall Ivey ; illustrated by Chuck Galey
      p. cm.
  Summary: One summer, Jay reads so many books that he turns into a
giant, and only when he begins to tell all the stories he has read does
he turn back into a normal eight-year-old boy.
  ISBN-13: 978-1-58980-372-5 (hardcover : alk. paper)
  [1. Books and reading--Fiction. 2. Giants--Fiction. 3. Storytelling--
Fiction.] I. Galey, Chuck, ill. II. Title.
  PZ7.I9516Jay 2007
  [E]--dc22

                                    2006031115

Printed in Singapore

Published by Pelican Publishing Company, Inc.
1000 Burmaster Street, Gretna, Louisiana 70053

Jay and the Bounty of Books

Jay's mother worried about all the time he spent watching television that summer. One day she switched the TV off and said, "Enough! Go outdoors now and play."

Jay went out and played but soon grew bored.

"Mom, it's time for 'The Robot Warriors.' And after that it's 'Super-Duper Pup.'"

Jay's mother shook her head and said, "An eight-year-old boy should not be bored. I will fix that for you."

She drove Jay to the library and helped him pick out books.

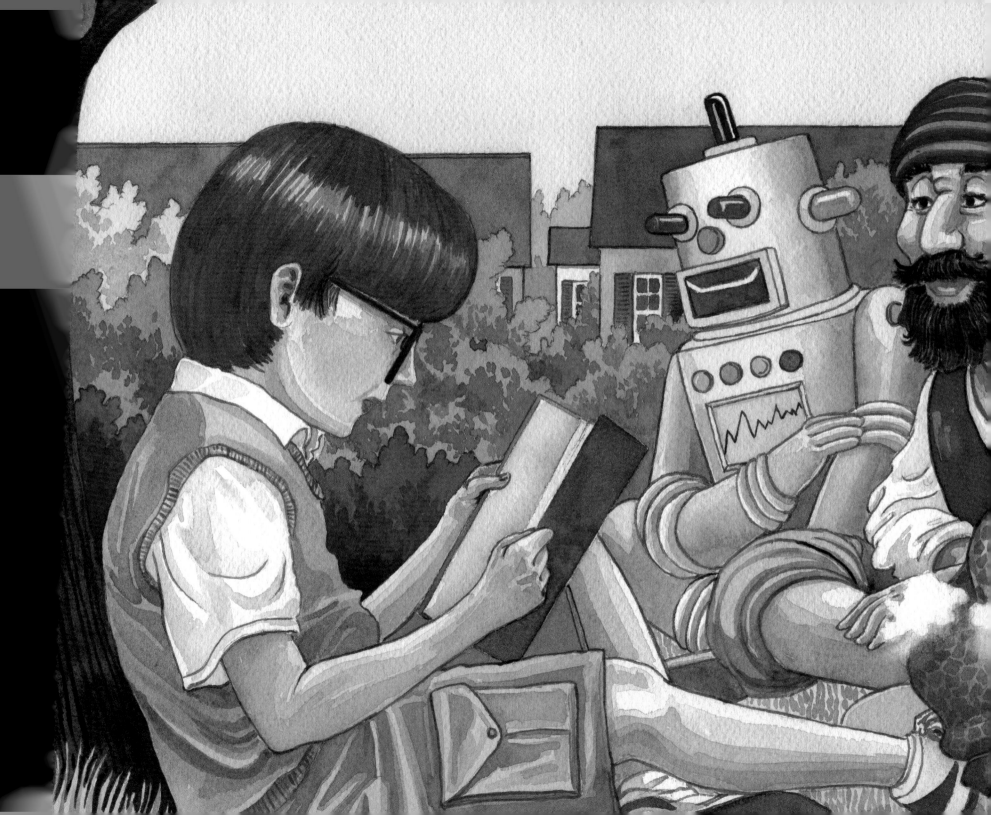

Jay took his books to the backyard and read about pirates and robots and green-necked dinosaurs with scarlet tongues and chimpanzees dancing on the moon. The books took him everywhere imaginable.

Jay burst back into the kitchen and shouted, "Mom!"

She looked up and wagged her finger. "Now, son, do not tell me you are bored with your books."

"Oh no, ma'am!" Jay exclaimed. "I love books. I want to read all the books in the world!"

The next day Jay's mother took him back to the library. They also visited the local bookstore. They returned, nearly toppling over with the books they carried in their arms, and took them to the backyard.

Hours went by, and Jay's mother had heard nothing from him. She went out to check on him but didn't find him on the blanket. All his books were there in discarded piles. She called his name and searched the yard. She began to worry.

Finally, from the woods behind their house, she heard, "Mom, here. I'm here!" She followed the sound of his voice into the woods. When Jay called from directly above her—"Mom, here I am!"—she nearly jumped out of her skin.

She knew she had heard her son's voice, but she did not see him. She looked around for him. "No, Mom, here. Up here!"

Jay's mother looked up with shock. It was Jay all right, but he was no longer a boy. Jay had somehow grown gigantic! His clothes and glasses had grown with him. She could not guess his height from where she stood. All she knew was that her son stood so high that he towered over the top of the highest tree. He was taller than their house and almost half as wide.

"Jay, what in the world has happened to you?"

"I don't know, Mom. I was reading all the books, and I fell asleep. When I woke up, here I was!"

Jay's mother told him to stay right there. She went back to the house and called his father at work. When she returned, Jay had come into the yard. Neighborhood children had gathered around, pointing at him and calling to him.

"I'll bet Jay's mother won't try to tell him what to do anymore," a little girl said.

Hearing this, Jay's mother gently touched her shoulder and replied, "Oh yes I will." Then she looked up at Jay. "I thought I told you to stay where you were."

"See, I told you!" the little girl said.

Soon Jay's father arrived, and behind him more people came to stare at Jay. The police came, and so did the firemen, with their lights flashing and their sirens wailing.

At the sight of them, Jay clapped his hands with delight. He reached down and picked up a police car as he would one of his own toys. The uniformed men scattered.

"No, no, no!" Jay's parents shouted together. "They're real!"

In no time Jay became the most famous little boy in the entire world. His picture was shown—on television!—and the newspapers reported the story of the young boy who read himself into gianthood. More and more people came to see him. The town was clogged with the curious from all over the world who stood and stared and pointed at Jay.

One afternoon, there emerged from this crowd a gentleman with a beard. The TV cameras zoomed in on him. The police stiffened into readiness should he mean Jay harm. He claimed to be an expert on all the strange things of the world. He said Jay was not the first young boy to whom this had happened. There had been others. And furthermore, he knew how to make Jay a little boy again.

"You do?" cried Jay's parents together. "Oh please do tell us."

"What?" the gentleman asked. "You don't like having a giant for a son?"

"Oh please tell us! We'll never find clothes to fit him nor a cereal bowl big enough."

"Ah yes," he sighed. "Just as I thought. So be it." He turned to Jay's mother. "In an interview that was broadcast on television, you said Jay, prior to becoming a giant, was out in the backyard reading books."

Jay's mother nodded. "Oh yes! Stacks and stacks. I lost count!"

The man nodded. "Just as in the other two cases I have cited. Reading has made a giant of Jay. Think of all the *story* he has in him! Imagine all the people those tales have let him meet and all the places they have taken him. These are experiences that will never be taken from him. Stories have made a giant of him!"

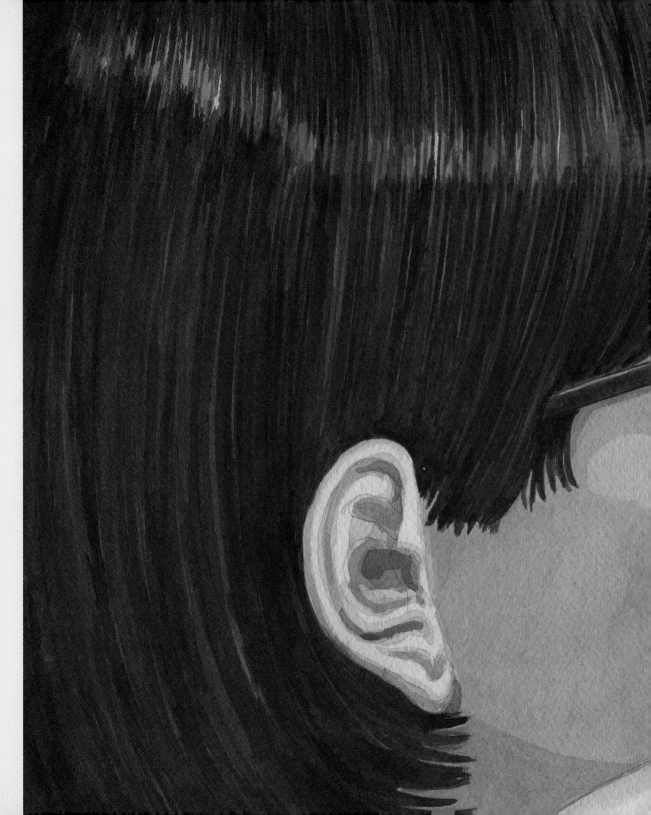

"But, sir, a little while ago you mentioned a possible solution to this problem. Could you talk a little more about that?" Jay's father prompted.

"If my study of these matters is correct, then Jay must give back all the stories he has taken from the books by telling them to everyone else." The man threw open his arms at the hundreds and thousands of people who circled Jay in his hometown. Then he pointed to the sky, swarming with helicopters and other aircraft, all beaming Jay's image around the world. No other storyteller ever had a more captive audience of this size! The gentleman turned quickly and pointed to Jay.

"Tell your tales, my boy!" he cried. "Give the world your stories!"

That is just what Jay did. He recounted tales of robots and dinosaurs, firemen and freight trains, pirates and acrobats, soldiers and sailors, and other little boys and little girls all over the world and from different points in time. As the force of his storytelling reduced him once again to the size of a little boy before the eyes of millions of spectators, his stories gave all of his listeners, man and woman, boy and girl, young and old, what they needed to become giants themselves—in their own way.